Branigan's Cat and the Halloween Ghost

For Alexander and Jezebel, two mythic cats.
S.K.

Text copyright © 1990 by Steven Kroll
Illustrations copyright © 1990 by Carolyn Ewing
Printed in the United States of America
First Edition

Library of Congress Cataloging-in-Publication Data
Kroll, Steven.
Branigan's cat and the Halloween ghost / written by Steven Kroll;
illustrated by Carolyn Ewing.
p.   cm.
Summary: Llewellyn the cat earns the villagers' respect when he
challenges the ghost of Martin Grimes on Halloween night.
ISBN 0-8234-0822-1
[1. Cats—Fiction.   2. Ghosts—Fiction.   3. Halloween—Fiction.]
I. Ewing, C. S., ill. II. Title.
PZ7.K9225Bq   1990
[E]—dc20   89-77509   CIP   AC
ISBN 0-8234-0822-1

Branigan's Cat and the Halloween Ghost

by Steven Kroll

illustrated by Carolyn Ewing

Holiday House/New York

John Branigan was a poor woodcutter. He lived in a small hut near a dark forest. All he had in the world was a big black cat called Llewellyn.

Llewellyn looked fierce, but he was really very gentle. He loved curling up in Branigan's lap. When Branigan scratched him behind the ears, he purred.

Branigan loved his cat so much that when he went into the village to sell his wood, he took Llewellyn with him. But each time the villagers saw how big the cat was and how fierce he looked, they fled to their homes in fear. Even the bravest knew black cats could bring bad luck.

Soon nobody would buy wood from Branigan. He had to go up to the mountains to find customers. But the mountain people were poor and could pay only half the price. When Branigan's efforts brought in barely enough for bread, he told Llewellyn, "I'm sorry, friend. I need to go back to the village to get more money for my wood. You're going to have to stay home."

The next morning, the morning of Halloween, Branigan set out for the village alone. That night, before he could return, a great rush of wind swept the hut.

Llewellyn was curled up in Branigan's favorite chair. His eyes popped open when he heard the wind. The ghost of an old man, dressed in rags and a dusty cape, hovered above him.

"I am Martin Grimes," said the ghost. "This hut belonged to me. Now, on Halloween night, I want it back."

Llewellyn arched his back. He bared his teeth and hissed.

Even the ghost was afraid. "You better watch out," he said. "You better get out of here."

Llewellyn leaped off the chair. He grabbed at the ghost, but the ghost darted away.

"Leave me alone," he said, "or you'll be in trouble."

Llewellyn chased Martin Grimes all over the hut. Finally the ghost grew angry. He knocked over the oil lamp and set the curtains on fire!

"That will teach you!" Grimes cackled as the flames leaped high.

The fire spread across the room. Llewellyn knew he couldn't stop it. As the flames licked at his fur, he fled into the forest.

For a long time he ran. It was very dark, but a strange, silvery light seemed to guide him along the path.

After many miles, a loud "Hooooooo!" stopped him in his tracks. He looked up. An owl with bright, golden eyes was staring down at him from a branch.

"I am guardian of the enchanted forest," the owl said. "If you follow the path and use well what I give you, you will come to no harm."

He dropped a necklace, a crown, and a sword to the ground. Llewellyn placed the necklace around his neck and the crown upon his head. He gripped the sword in his teeth.

"Go in peace," said the owl.

Llewellyn strode on through the forest. Before long, he came to a roaring waterfall. He was wondering how to continue when a bridge magically appeared.

Llewellyn started across. When he reached the middle, the bridge broke in half. Llewellyn was left dangling by one paw above the raging torrent!

At that moment, a serpent reared up out of the water. But Llewellyn was too quick for him. With his free paw, he grabbed the sword out of his mouth and cut off the monster's head!

The serpent fell back into the water. The two halves of the bridge became one again, and Llewellyn crossed onto dry land.

The strange, silvery light continued to guide Llewellyn, and the path held his feet. When he came around a corner, a gigantic lion was blocking his way.

The lion looked ten times as fierce as Llewellyn. "I am going to eat you," he said. "You will make an excellent dinner."

"But wait," said Llewellyn. "You are the king of beasts. Before you dine, would you not like to try on my crown?"

He removed the crown from his head and placed it on the lion. The lion pulled a mirror from behind a tree and began admiring himself. Llewellyn turned and ran off down the path.

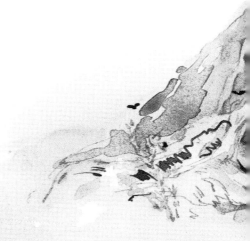

The path grew narrower and then wider. It went down a hill and up another. At the very top was a gate. On either side stood two gray cats with swords.

The two cats dove at Llewellyn! One sat on his stomach. The other held a sword at his throat!

"Wait!" said Llewellyn. He grabbed his necklace and held it out for them to see.

The guards gasped. They knew the wearer of the necklace had the right to pass. They leaped back and threw open the gate.

The path was now paved with gold. Llewellyn walked until he came to a clearing. On a throne bathed in light was a big black cat very like himself.

Removing the necklace from Llewellyn's neck, the cat said, "I am glad you have come. I have something for you."

He held out a silver wand. "You have shown courage, and with this, you will return to the village and face the ghost of Martin Grimes."

"Yes, Your Highness," said Llewellyn.

He took the silver wand in his mouth and raced down the golden path. The gate opened, and he hurried back the way he had come. In no time he had reached the edge of the forest.

He ran to Branigan's hut. It had been rebuilt, but no one was there. He dashed to the village and found a large crowd in the main square.

In the enchanted forest, only a day had passed. In the world, an entire year had gone by, and it was once again Halloween night. The ghost of Martin Grimes was flying around the square. "Give me back my hut!" he wailed, "or I'll burn down the village!"

Llewellyn climbed to a rooftop. As the ghost flew by, he held up the silver wand. The ghost disappeared with a loud pop! The people in the square threw their hats in the air and cheered.

Llewellyn climbed back down to the street. Branigan rushed over, picked him up, and hugged him.

The villagers picked up Branigan and paraded him and Llewellyn around the square. Then they carried them both down Main Street and out to Branigan's hut.

"Branigan," said the mayor, "we want you to know how grateful we are to Llewellyn. He will always be welcome in our village."

"Thank you, Mayor," said Branigan. "I know Llewellyn will be glad to hear that. He never did anyone a wrong, and I've missed him for a long time."

Llewellyn put his paws around Branigan's neck and purred. Branigan carried him inside. Together they fell asleep in the woodcutter's favorite chair.